W9-DEW-879

Readers will also enjoy:

DIRKLE SMAT
INSIDE MOUNT FLATBOTTOM

DIRKLE SMAT
AND THE FLYING STATUE

Lynn Garthwaite

And The
Flying Statue

LYNN D. GARTHWAITE

Illustrated by Craig Howarth

CASTLE KEEP PRESS
James A. Rock & Company, Publishers
Rockville, Maryland

Dirkle Smat and the Flying Statue by Lynn D. Garthwaite
Illustrated by Craig Howarth

CASTLE KEEP PRESS
is an imprint of JAMES A. ROCK & CO., PUBLISHERS

Dirkle Smat and the Flying Statue
copyright ©2007 by Lynn D. Garthwaite

Special contents of this edition copyright ©2007
by James A. Rock & Co., Publishers

Address comments and inquiries to:
CASTLE KEEP PRESS
James A. Rock & Company, Publishers
9710 Traville Gateway Drive, #305
Rockville, MD 20850

E-mail:
jrock@rockpublishing.com   lrock@rockpublishing.com
Internet URL: www.rockpublishing.com

ISBN: 978-1-59663-553-1

Library of Congress Control Number: 2007921591

Printed in the United States of America

First Edition 2007

Cover and interior illustrations by Craig Howarth

http://home.wol.co.za/~20291447/

Also in this series:
Dirkle Smat Inside Mount Flatbottom
Dirkle Smat and the Viking Shield

**Check out Fun Stuff at
www.dirklesmat.com**

*To my Mom
who has always encouraged
my imagination and believed
that I could do anything.
Thanks Mom!*

Chapter One

The crackle of the Lumleyline woke Dirkle Smat out of a sound nap. Dirkle didn't often fall asleep in the middle of the day, but on this warm, sunny Saturday afternoon the backyard hammock just felt too inviting. Minutes after he lay down, his eyes closed and he dozed.

It was Bean Lumley calling on the Lumleyline which was his own invention. It was similar to a hardware store walkie talkie but the Lumleyline was attached to a small monitor on which people could

see each
other
while they
talked.

"Dirkle,
are we still
meeting at the
clubhouse this af-
ternoon?" asked Bean.

Dirkle was relieved that Bean had called
and awakened him. He might have slept
through an Explorer's Club meeting!

"You bet," Dirkle replied. "Round up the
troops and I'll see you there at three."

The Explorer's Club clubhouse was actually a small bus that had been abandoned at the edge of the woods. Years ago, the bus drove off the road during a thunderstorm and, since the town didn't have a tow truck big enough to drag it out of the ditch, the bus had sat there ever since. Dirkle and his friends converted it into a clubhouse and the fast growing trees and shrubs had now practically covered it, hiding it from anyone driving by.

Dirkle double-checked to see if his brother Quid was in the yard before he mounted his roto-scooter to head out. Bean had invented the roto-scooter for his own use but the other Explorers had been so envious that they asked Bean to make one for each of them.

Whistling the theme from his favorite cartoon, Dirkle rode down the street and turned the corner.

Two miles later, as he approached the clubhouse, Dirkle was surprised to see Quid standing in the tall grass alongside Toonie Oobles, Bean Lumley, and Fiddy Bublob. *Yoips,* thought Dirkle. *That kid sure seems to always know when we're meeting.*

Dirkle pulled his roto-scooter into the parking spaces they had created on the other side of the bus. Each Explorer had his name on a piece of tag board taped onto the bus to mark his special parking place. Being the leader of the Club, Dirkle's space was up front. Quid had scribbled his own name on a piece of tag board and taped it to the back of the bus.

"Everyone is here," Dirkle said with authority. "Let's call the meeting to order."

Chapter Two

"You've all heard the rumors," began Dirkle. Each Explorer sat in his or her assigned seat on the bus while Dirkle stood at the front by the driver's seat.

"Townspeople have been whispering about a strange sighting in the sky late at night a couple of times this year, and no one knows what to make of it."

"My neighbors said it looked like a flying *horse*," reported Toonie. "They thought it looked just like the statue of Pegasus which sits in the town square."

"Those are the same reports I've heard," replied Bean. "That's why we brought everyone here to discuss it."

Fiddy had a confused look on his face. "How can a horse *fly?* They don't have wings."

Bean stood and opened a large book of Greek myths he'd brought with him.

"In ancient times, people believed there was a flying horse called a Pegasus. If you look at the picture, you'll see that it does have wings and it does fly. By the way, if you have more than one Pegasus, they're called Pegasi," Bean explained.

"Pegasi is the plural of Pegasus?" asked Fiddy.

Bean nodded.

Everyone took a turn looking at the book and the picture of the mythical beast.

"I've seen the statue in the center of town," added Quid. "But it's made of marble! I don't see how it could take off."

"That's what we're going to find out,"

said Dirkle. "Bean and I have been talking about it and we have a theory. We believe that somehow the full moon can bring the statue to life."

"That's right," continued Bean. "I checked my calendar for the dates of the rumored sightings, and they match up with the weather service reports of a full moon. We're ready to test our theory tonight because there is going to be a full moon."

There was a feeling of excitement in the air as the Explorers discussed their new mission. Plans had to be made. Supplies had to be brought. Watches needed to be synchronized. They all agreed to meet back at Fiddy's before sunset with the cover story that they would be camping in a tent in Fiddy's backyard.

The plan was to camp until just before midnight. Then they would head into town to see if a marble horse can *really* fly.

Chapter Three

Fiddy's backyard was perfect for camping because the long yard swooped down to the edge of a small pond and a large field that served as homes for a variety of animals and insects. The night air was filled with all kinds of wild sounds. It was a little spooky listening to the crickets and the owls singing their late night songs. Sitting in the huge tent with flashlights, the Explorers planned their night's adventure.

Bean reached into his duffel bag and pulled out a tangled mess of leather straps.

As he spread them out on the floor of the tent, he explained his latest invention.

"I fabricated a special harness that will hold us onto the statue's back if she truly does begin to fly. There is a seat belt for each of us and two straps that will go under the Pegasus and snap onto the other side."

"That's cool," said Toonie. "It's like a giant saddle for all five of us!"

Fiddy picked up the harness and looked it over. "Do we know if the statue is actually big enough to hold all of us?"

"We'll know soon enough," replied Dirkle. "It's 11:15 and time to head to the Town Square. If our calculations are right, we'll need to be strapped onto the statue by midnight."

"I brought a carrot to feed Peggy," said

Toonie and they all chuckled at the nick-
name she chose for the statue. "I figure if
she's made of marble, she doesn't get much
to eat."

"Good thinking," smiled Dirkle. "I brought
a compass and a map. I'm going to try to
chart our flight to see where we end up."

"I brought snacks," said Fiddy, bringing
a round of applause from everyone. "For
us," he added, "not the horse."

Then Quid noticed a wool scarf that
Fiddy had wrapped around his
shoulders.

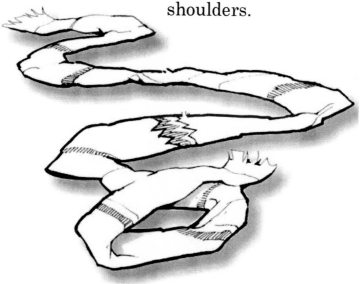

"Fiddy," Quid exclaimed. "it's almost 90 degrees outside. Why are you wearing a wool scarf?"

"I'm just thinking it might get cold up in the clouds if we really do get off the ground tonight," Fiddy answered. "I want to be prepared."

Chapter Four

Town Square was about twenty minutes away by bike, but by *roto-scooter* the Explorers were there in less than ten minutes. As they expected, the area was deserted since everyone was home, probably sleeping soundly. The only sound came from the bullfrogs in the pond behind the courthouse.

Quid helped Bean carry the heavy harness over to the feet of the statue and looked up in awe at the massive beast. He had never been this close to it before and was amazed at how large it was.

"We should have brought a ladder," he exclaimed. "How are we going to get up on this thing?"

"We'll hoist each other up to the wing and hop onto the statue's back from there. Then, the last guy will get pulled up by the others," said Dirkle, who had it all planned out. "Let's get this harness on her and get started."

It took several tries, but the five of them were finally able to throw the saddle part of the harness on top of the statue, leaving the long straps dangling underneath. Bean grabbed the dangling ends and pulled them under the statue's belly. Then, while Dirkle lifted him up, he fastened both belt edges to the saddle on the other side and pulled them tight.

The straps held firmly to the underside of the horse and kept the saddle on top tightly in place.

"Is everyone ready?" asked Dirkle.

Toonie stuffed the carrot in her pocket and nodded. Bean and Fiddy put their hands together and lifted Dirkle up to the statue's wing where he hopped to the front seat in the saddle on Peggy's back. Next came Toonie who found her spot behind Dirkle who was already snapping on his seat belt.

Quid helped Fiddy lift Bean to his place behind Toonie. Then, with Bean's helping hand from above, he gave Fiddy a boost to the top. Now it was up to Fiddy, alone, to pull Quid up with no help from below. But, since Quid was the lightest of the group, Fiddy managed with only a few grunts.

Bean looked around at the group. "Everyone buckle the seat belts and pull them *tight*. We can't have anyone wiggling around during flight."

They all adjusted their seat belts until they were good and snug when, suddenly, the statue let out a loud *snort*.

Chapter
Five

"Yoips!" said Dirkle, startled by the sound. The other Explorers each grabbed the person in front of them and the statue started to *move*. Dirkle could only grab the front end of the saddle as the marble they were sitting on slowly changed into the strong, sturdy, warm body of a horse. Its muscles moved and twitched, as if stretching after a long sleep, and its long proud neck raised up toward the sky.

"I think something's happening," cried

Fiddy, who suddenly wished he had stayed back in the tent.

"Everyone secure themselves tightly to the harness and prepare for liftoff," shouted Bean. "We don't know quite how this is going to work!"

The horse's incredible wings began to slowly rise and fall, feeling the air and ruffling the dust off its feathers. One of its hooves made a thunderous sound as it rose and fell back on the platform and the shaggy mane on the back of its neck shook.

"I'm thinking we should have *watched* the first time—before strapping ourselves on," suggested Quid, his voice revealing a slight tremble.

"Then we would have had to wait a whole month," Dirkle shouted back over the sound of the horse's snort. "I wouldn't want to wait that long."

And, indeed, the five Explorers didn't have to wait another minute. Suddenly the living, breathing statue leapt off the plat-

form and cantered across the courthouse
lawn. Her wings began to flap with extra
urgency and, just as they reached the edge
of the grass, the ground fell away beneath
them and they were flying.

"I can't believe it, I can't believe it,"
shouted Toonie, her pigtails falling straight
back behind her with the wind. "We're flying!"

"I can't believe it either," mumbled Fiddy, his face turning a pale shade of green as his stomach did flip-flops.

But, after a couple of minutes, the Explorers began to get used to the feeling of sitting atop a flying statue. They began to relax and look around. Beneath them the ground kept dropping away as the Pegasus flew higher and higher into the night sky.

"No one's going to believe THIS one!" laughed Dirkle. "We must be a mile high!"

Bean shouted above the sound of the air rushing by. "I brought an altimeter. I can tell you exactly how high we are." He reached into his pocket and brought out the small instrument.

"We are currently 4,025 feet in the air. When we reach 5,280 feet, we'll be a mile high."

They all felt like cowboys in the highest rodeo in history. Despite the fear, their faces sported huge grins and their eyes were full of wonder.

"We're above the clouds now," they heard Quid say from behind. "I wonder where we're ..."

Quid never finished his sentence because, at that exact moment, his seat belt snapped loose and he felt like he was about to be thrown from the back of the flying horse.

Chapter Six

"Quid!" screamed Fiddy, who heard the snap and felt Quid start to fall away from him. He turned his head to see Quid sliding backward, off of the saddle, both fists holding tight to Fiddy's shirt.

The others craned their necks and gasped! Strapped to the harness as they were, none of them (except Fiddy) could reach Quid. They watched, helplessly, as Dirkle's little brother hung on tight.

The wind felt stronger to Quid now that he wasn't attached to the saddle and it whipped his hair around as he fought to hang onto Fiddy.

He gripped Fiddy's shirt with every ounce of energy he had! Now Quid concentrated on pulling himself forward. He wished, briefly, that he'd done more pull-ups to strengthen his arms. But, like a true Explorer, he quickly chased that thought away and concentrated on the predicament he was in.

"I'll pull you back on," shouted Fiddy, as he reached behind and grabbed Quid's legs. With both boys now pulling as hard as they could, Quid was finally safe again, sitting snugly behind Fiddy on the harness that Bean had made.

"Just hang on to Fiddy until we land," Bean shouted. "I can't fix the harness in mid-flight."

But Fiddy had a better idea.

"Here, take my scarf," he shouted to Quid, "Now *wrap* it around your back," he instructed. "I'll tie it around my waist. That way you'll be attached to me and, since I'm buckled in, we'll both be safe."

Quid did as Fiddy suggested and soon the long, wool scarf was wrapped around both boys, securing them tightly to each other. Everyone kept looking back with worried faces, glad to see Quid was safely attached to his friend.

Dirkle pulled his compass out of his pocket and looked at it with confusion.

"I was hoping to chart our course to determine where we're going," he shouted back to his fellow Explorers. "But the compass has gone crazy. The dial is just spinning around and around, out of control."

He looked ahead, over the neck of the flying statue, just in time to see the clouds open up and reveal the land below them.

All five Explorers let out a collective gasp. Their eyes were wide with wonder as they gazed at the land below them.

"We're above some magical fantasyland," whispered Toonie.

Chapter Seven

One moment earlier they had been flying in the dark night sky. Now, suddenly, as the Pegasus dipped below the clouds, sunshine flooded the skies, lighting up the ground below.

Everything around them was a lush green. They could see rolling hills and streams meandering through the land. Brilliant colors dotted the landscape and, as they flew closer to the ground, they could see that the colors were actually beautiful flowers. Thousands of flowers of every possible shade. Some were splashed with colors they didn't think they had ever seen before.

And, wandering amongst the flowers and the grass, were hundreds of *other* Pegasi—all in their own amazing colors and all with proud wings tucked close to their sides.

"Look," said Toonie. "Peggy has changed color!"

Sure enough, the white marble of the horse they rode had turned to a soft rose with silver sparkles scattered throughout. Her mane and tail were a brilliant, deep royal blue, like the color of the ocean around an exotic island.

Colors were everywhere and the air was fresh and clean.

"This is beautiful," whispered Bean. "I wonder where we are."

"There's no way to tell," replied Dirkle. "My compass seems to be broken and I can't even say what direction we flew."

The touchdown was so smooth they didn't even realize they had landed until they felt the muscles in Peggy's flanks move beneath them as she galloped across the grass. When she finally stopped, near the other Pegasi, she bent her head to graze on the grass. The Explorers unfastened their seat belts and slid to the soft ground.

Dirkle turned to Quid who was still a little shaken from his flying adventure. "I'm sure glad you're okay Quid. You gave me a big scare there."

"I was a *little* scared, too" Quid replied, "but Fiddy's scarf worked great."

Dirkle gave his brother a quick hug and rubbed his head. "You're a tough little guy," he said with a laugh.

"Help me unfasten this harness, Quid, and we'll see what happened with your belt." Bean stood on one side of the great horse while Quid stood on the other. Together they unhooked the bottom of the harness and pulled it to the ground.

Toonie pulled the carrot from her pocket and offered it to Peggy, who took it eagerly and ate it up.

"Wow, this place is amazing," observed Dirkle, as he looked all around them. "Once a month, all the Pegasi around the world must meet here and stretch their legs. What a break it must be from being a marble statue on all the other days of the month."

"This is amazing. They keep changing color!" Fiddy gasped. "Look, Peggy went from that reddish color to a soft yellow. The other ones keep changing too."

It was true. As they gazed at the herd, their colors changed and alternately brightened and softened. Toonie noticed that odd-looking birds would land on the backs of the Pegasi and then take off and flitter around the herd. Butterflies the size of dinner plates played among the flowers.

"I figured out what happened with the harness," reported Bean. "The strap on that last belt hadn't been completely closed where it connected to the saddle. It must have pulled open and almost sent Quid flying."

Dirkle looked at the harness and could see that the buckle was hanging open. It took just a moment for Bean to secure it to the saddle again and a quick test assured him that it was solidly attached.

"You won't have any problem on the return trip, Quid," assured Bean. "We'll use that scarf to attach you to Fiddy again— just in case."

But when Quid and Bean turned around

to replace the harness they stopped short and stared. Which of these rainbow, color-changing Pegasi was *their* Peggy?

Chapter Eight

"Uh-oh," said Quid.

"What's the matter?" asked Toonie as she joined the group. "Do you need help with the harness?"

Quid and Bean exchanged glances. Bean gulped nervously. He turned to his fellow Explorers.

"Um ...," said Bean, "Can anyone tell the *difference* between these flying horses?"

"Yoips!" said Dirkle, who immediately realized what Bean was saying. He looked around. The Pegasi were wandering about and pawing the ground. Dirkle searched frantically among them for a familiar sign.

"Not only can't I tell the difference because they keep changing colors," said Dirkle, frowning. "But it looks like they're getting *restless*—like they're getting ready to take off and fly back to where they came from."

No one spoke for a moment as they realized their predicament.

Finally Fiddy whispered what all of them were thinking.

"If we get on the wrong one, who knows where we'll end up?"

All around them colorful Pegasi were prancing restlessly. There was a feeling in the air that time was running out. The Explorers knew they had to find their statue soon if they were going to get home.

Quid surveyed the situation. "I think it would be better to get on the wrong one," he offered, "than not to get on *any* horse.

Then we'd be stranded here until the next full moon!"

Suddenly Toonie grabbed Dirkle's shirt sleeve and pointed excitedly. "Look, look!" she cried.

Everyone turned to see where Toonie was pointing.

One of the beautiful horses had just turned toward them and, in the corner of her mouth, hanging on the edge of her lip, was a tiny piece of a bright orange carrot.

"That's Peggy! That's her! That's the carrot I was feeding her."

"Thank goodness she didn't lick her lips," said Bean, smiling.

Having spotted their ride home, the Explorers happily set to work, securing the harness back on Peggy. Then, one by one, they hitched each other back up to their place on the saddle.

"Is your seat belt working okay, Quid?" Dirkle called back to his little brother.

"Yep, it seems just fine. But I'm strapping myself onto Fiddy with the scarf and holding tight with both hands—just in case."

They all looked on in amazement as, one by one, the Pegasi galloped across the grass and lifted into the air with their big powerful wings. The Explorers felt the thrill of take-off again as their own horse, with five riders on her back, glided back into the night air and quickly reached the top of the clouds.

The beautiful fantasyland disappeared beneath them and they were once again flying through the dark night sky.

Chapter Nine

The five kids were cold and tired by the time they landed in the town square. Peggy touched down silently on the grass beside the courthouse and walked to the platform that was built to hold the statue. As soon as she was in place on the platform, the Explorers could feel her skin and muscles begin to harden as she began to turn back into marble.

The Explorers quickly slid off the horse, unhooked the harness and pulled it to the ground behind them.

Then they stood back and watched the final transformation. Peggy's colors gradually faded and disappeared. Finally she became the white marble statue that they had known all their lives.

"Yoips," said Dirkle, because he was amazed.

"I wonder if this happens to the statues of dragons, too?" said Quid.

"I wouldn't want to ever find out. Can you imagine being near a dragon that could really breathe fire?" Fiddy asked.

Just as they turned to walk away, Dirkle saw something that made him smile. The tiny piece of carrot that had clung on Peggy's lips broke away from the now hardened mouth of the statue and fell to the ground.

"This was certainly the ride of our lives," reported Bean.

"So far," answered Dirkle. "So far."

About the Author

Lynn Garthwaite lives in Bloomington, Minnesota with her husband and two sons.

Make Your Own Explorer's Club

Members:

_____

_____

_____

_____

_____

Members:

Equipment:

Adventures:

_____

_____

_____

_____

_____

_____

9 781596 635531